Please return/renew this item by the last date shown.
Library items may also be renewed by phone on
030 33 33 1234 (24hours) or via our website

www.cumbria.gov.uk/libraries

Cumbria Libraries

CLIC
Interactive Catalogue

Ask for a CLIC password

First published in paperback in Great Britain 2018
by Egmont UK Limited
The Yellow Building, 1 Nicholas Road, London W11 4AN

Text copyright © 2018 Sam Watkins
Illustrations copyright © 2018 Vicky Barker
The moral rights of the author and illustrator have been asserted

ISBN 978 1 4052 8424 0

www.egmont.co.uk

65067/1

A CIP catalogue record for this title is available from the British Library

Printed and bound in Great Britain by the CPI Group

Stay safe online. Any website addresses listed in this book are
correct at the time of going to print. However, Egmont is not
responsible for content hosted by third parties.
Please be aware that online content can be subject to change and
websites can contain content that is unsuitable for children. We advise
that all children are supervised when using the internet.

CONTENTS

Week 1
Lend a Fin!   11

Week 2
The Happy Abyss Retired Sharks'   65
Home

Week 3
The Best Party Ever!   123

PHEE-WEEEEE, it's me again, humans. I'm having a whale of a time, because it's the SUMMER HOLIDAYS! This year it's doubly exciting because I am also going to **Sea Trouts**. My best friends, Ozzie Octopus and Myrtle Turtle, have been going for a while and they persuaded me to join.

Sea Trouts is an evening club for kids that's on every Monkfishday night. We do loads of fintastic stuff like playing games and singing songs, and last week we even did scientific experiments! The experiments were mega-cool so I tried one out at home. Unfortunately it sort of exploded all over the kitchen. ☺

Mum totally flipped out and Aunt Ditzy had to come round to calm her down. Aunt Ditzy brought a book to help Mum called **Inspiring Thoughts for Stressed Sea Life**. The first Inspiring Thought is: 'Just keep swimming, just keep swimming.'

I didn't think that was very inspiring, but I've decided that I'm going to write a Thought of the Day every day in my new diary. My first one is:

Thought of the Day: ALWAYS MAKE A SPLASH!

WEEK 1:
Lend a Fin!

MONKFISHDAY

Sea Trouts tonight, yippeeeee! Ozzie and Myrtle came to pick me up. We were all wearing our uniforms – neck scarves held on by wooden rings called **woggles**. When we got to the Trout Hut there were already loads of Sea Trouts there, screeching and chasing each other around.

'SEA TROUTS – FREEZE!'

Everyone froze as our leader, Brown Trout, swam out. Her main talent is Scowling Disapprovingly.

13

'TO YOUR

SHOALS!'

Everyone shot

into their Shoals.

There are four Shoals

– Blennies, Anchovies,

Guppies and Minnows. Ozzie, Myrtle and

I are the Minnows.

'Before we begin, it's time to change Shoal

Leaders,' Brown Trout said. 'The new leaders

are as follows . . .'

She held up a list.

'Blennies – Chris Codling. Anchovies – Lyla

Longfin. Guppies – Reggie Ray. And Minnows . . .

Darcy Dolphin.'

'Yippee!' I squeaked, quite loudly I think

because Brown Trout gave me one of her

Disapproving Scowls. I shut my mouth, but inside my head my brain was doing a happy dance. Myrtle had been Shoal Leader for **aaaages**. Well, two weeks anyway. Now *I* was the boss and could tell the others what to do for a change! I would be quite a strict boss, I decided, like Brown Trout. I twisted my face up and pulled my eyebrows together like she does when she's being particularly disapproving.

'What are you doing with your face, Darcy?' Ozzie whispered.

I stopped.
'Nothing.'

Myrtle giggled.

'You looked like you ate a rotten sea slug!'

'I am Shoal Leader now . . .' I began. But Brown Trout was beckoning.

'Shoal Leaders, over here!' As I swam over, I bumped into Reggie Ray, the new Guppies leader.

'Oops, sorry!' I said.

Reggie glared. 'Watch it, big nose!'

Big nose?! I was so surprised I couldn't think of ANYTHING to say! I tried to think of something. Something really clever . . . barnacle brain? Squid lips?

'FLAT FACE!' I exclaimed, then realised that Brown Trout was staring at me.

'Pardon, Darcy?'

'She asked you what the Sea Trout motto is,' whispered Lyla Longfin.

'I mean, um, Lend a Fin,' I mumbled.

'Yes,' Brown Trout said. 'And that means being **helpful** to others. Now, this month is Lend a Fin month, which means you are all going to be extra-helpful. At the end of the month there is a prize for the most helpful Shoal.' She held up a gleaming, golden ring. 'The Golden Woggle.'

The Golden Woggle

Everyone gasped. I stared. The Golden Woggle was beautiful. I saw Reggie Ray looking greedily at it.

Brown Trout was handing out cards. 'After you've helped someone, give them your card and ask them to tick off one Help Point. They can tick off more if they think you've been extra-helpful.'

I took our Help Points card back to Ozzie and Myrtle. They started talking excitedly about what sort of things we could do. I just couldn't stop looking over at the Golden Woggle.

We had to win it. We WOULD win it!

Thought of the Day: There can be only ONE winner of the Golden Woggle.

TUNASDAY

I got up at 5 am and started being **helpful**
immediately.

First I did some hoovering. But I
accidentally hoovered up my little brother
Diddy's favourite soft toy, Sharkie. Diddy's
screams brought Mum and Dad hurtling
in from the bedroom – they thought I was
murdering Diddy! Dad had to shake the vacfish
until Sharkie fell out. He'd lost an eye, some
teeth and most of his stuffing, but apart from
that he was okay.

Mum collapsed on the sofa. 'Please, Darcy, no more hoovering!'

'But I need Help Points!' I showed Mum the Help Points card. Mum groaned and clutched her head. I thought maybe she was coming down with something.

'You look ill,' I said, patting her fin. 'You should go back to bed. I'll do all the housework today.'

'I'm fine, sweetiefins. It's just – a little early.' She yawned. 'I need a cup of sea . . .'

I leapt up. 'I'll make it!'

'Darcy, wait . . .'

'It's no trouble . . .'

I whizzed into the kitchen, Remy on my tail. What did I need? Seabags, milk, sugar. The seabags were right at the back of a cupboard and I had to chuck loads of things out to get to them. I dropped the milk when I got it out of the fridge, but that was okay, Mum would just have to have black sea. I opened every single cupboard and pulled everything out but couldn't find the sugar anywhere. Then I opened the top cupboard.

No sugar. But there WAS a big stack of Jiggling Jellies!

My mouth started watering. Jiggling Jellies are my favourite sweets. They were very untidily stacked, though.

I decided to tidy the cupboard up.

I'm not sure how, but I somehow managed to tidy every single Jiggling Jelly in the cupboard into my mouth.

'DARCY! WHAT IS GOING ON?'

Mum was at the door, looking horrified. The kitchen looked like an underwater volcano had erupted in it. In the middle of the mess, guzzling the food I'd thrown out in my search for the sugar, was Remy. He wagged his tail at Mum, and burped loudly.

I quickly slurped in the **Jiggling Jelly** that was hanging out of my mouth.

'It's okay Mum, I'll tidy up,' I said. 'And then I'll make breakfast . . .'

Mum went a very funny colour and started twitching. She said that the most helpful thing

I could do would be to not help any more, and that if I managed that she would give me a Help Point.

'But Mum . . .'

'NO BUTS!'

Thought of the Day: Never argue with a parent who is a funny colour and/or twitching.

WHALESDAY

'Can I help you today, Mum?' I pleaded at
breakfast. 'I *really* need Help Points.'

Mum started twitching again.

'I know, why don't you see if Ozzie's mum
needs any help?' Dad said quickly.

I decided to call for Myrtle first, and then
we swam round to Ozzie's shipwreck, The
Lucky Gull. Ozzie's mum had gone out.

'She's helping gran with her shopping,'
Ozzie said.

DING! I had a **tidal
brainwave**.

'WE can help old ladyfish with their shopping! We'll wait outside the supermarket and carry their bags home for them!'

Myrtle and Ozzie wanted to wait for Ozzie's mum. I reminded them that I was Shoal Leader and they had to do what I said.

We swam to Fishco, the biggest supermarket in town. As we got there I saw Reggie Ray hovering around by the doors, with two more Sea Trouts.

'What are the Guppies doing here?' I said crossly.

Ozzie gulped. 'I have a bad feeling about this –'

At that moment a little old ladyfish came swimming through the doors, carrying two full shopping bags.

'Minnows – GO!' I shouted, diving towards
the ladyfish. But Reggie was quicker.

'Can I help you with those bags, madam?'
said Reggie.

The ladyfish blinked in surprise.

'I'll help you!' I said loudly, darting round
Reggie and grabbing one of the bags.

'Hey!' Reggie tried to grab it off me. Suddenly the other Guppies dived in, all of them trying to grab the bag. Then . . .

'OW!'

The old ladyfish whacked me on the head with the other bag!

'I'll have that back, thank you!' She scurried away, muttering some not very

ladyfishlike things under her breath. The Guppies swam off too, sniggering.

'Darcy! Are you okay?' Ozzie and Myrtle dashed over. Ozzie had turned a shocking pink (he changes colour when he gets stressed).

I groaned. 'My head hurts! Is there a giant lump?'

Myrtle said she couldn't see one. Then Ozzie said that old ladyfish were too **dangerous** and we should go back to his shipwreck and wait for his mum.

'Well, all right,' I said. 'But it's ... wait – look over there!'

An old turtle was waiting to cross a road.

'Darcy, is this a good idea?' Ozzie said.

'Yes! Come on!'

I zoomed over to the turtle, keeping an eye out for lurking Guppies.

'We'll help you, sir!' I took the turtle's flipper. He looked a bit startled, but I had to be quick in case Reggie Ray showed up. Streams of fast-moving fish were whizzing along the road in both directions.

'After this one . . . GO!'

I yanked the turtle out into the road.

HOOOOONK! A whale shark swerved to avoid us. Then **SCREEEEECH!** A school of mackerel coming the other way screeched to a halt. Behind me I could hear Ozzie and Myrtle saying 'Sorry, really sorry . . .'

When we got to the other side of the road the turtle collapsed in a quivering heap.

'There you go,' I said, cheerily. 'Safely across the road!'

The turtle looked up at me. 'But I didn't WANT to cross the road,' he quavered. 'I was just having a rest!'

Aaaargh. No Help Points there, then. ☺

This helping thing is harder than I thought!

Thought of the Day: Just because a turtle is waiting by a road doesn't mean he wants to cross it.

TURTLESDAY

We needed a plan to get a load of Help Points,
so I decided to call a Helpers Meeting. We had
to go to Myrtle's because she was babysitting

her twin brothers, Tyler
and Trent. From the
moment I arrived
they wouldn't leave
me alone.

'Daaarrrrcy, why don't you have a shell?'

'Daaarrrrcy, do dolphins lay eggs?'

'Daaarrrrcy, why have you got a hole on your back?'

In the end Myrtle put them in front of the TV so we could start our meeting. *Octopirates* was on. The main character is Captain Tentacles, whose catchphrase is 'Yo ho hum!' Small fry think it's hilarious.

As the twins went quiet, I grabbed some paper and a pen and wrote, 'Helpers Meeting'.

'Now, is everyone here?' I said. 'Where is Ozzie Octopus?'

'He said he was going to be a bit late,' said Myrtle.

'Hmmm.' I wrote, 'Ozzie Octopus – LATE'.

'Why are you writing that down?' asked Myrtle.

'You have to write everything down in meetings,' I said.

'Now, what are our ideas for getting loads of Help Points?'

I looked at Myrtle. There was a long pause.

'We could tidy our bedrooms?' she said finally.

'Good idea,' I said. 'But we need something where we can get squillions of Help Points. We didn't get any yesterday! We need to THINK BIG.'

I wrote down: 'THINK BIG'.

It was really hard to think big with the TV yo-ho-humming away. Then there was a sudden burst of music as *Octopirates* ended and the twins hurled themselves on me.

'YO HO HUM!!! Be our pirate ship, Daaaarcy!'

Myrtle groaned. 'We'll never get anything done now! The only person who can keep the twins quiet is Captain Tentacles –'

The doorbell rang.

'I'll get it,' I said, shaking Tyler and Trent off and swimming to the door.

It was Ozzie. He looked a bit pink. 'Where've you been?' I asked.

'Sorry,' he said. 'I had to go to yoga with Mum – she says it's good for my tentacles . . .'

Tentacles . . . Sploosh – **BRAINWAVE!**

'Wait here,' I told Ozzie. I went back into the living room where the twins were now swordfish-fighting on the sofa.

36

'Have you got a pirate costume?' I asked
Myrtle.

'The twins have,' she said. 'They're
obsessed with pirates.' She pointed at a pirate
hat and eye-patch lying on the floor. I took
them out to Ozzie.

'Here, put these on.'

He looked at them suspiciously. 'Why?'

'Please – I can't explain now . . .'

Ozzie rolled his eyes, but he put the hat on and pulled the patch over his eye. I pulled him into the living room.

'Tyler, Trent – there's someone here to see you!'

The twins stopped fighting and peered over.

I nudged Ozzie. 'Say "Yo ho hum",' I whispered.

'Yo ho hum,' he mumbled. The twins shrieked in glee.

'Captain Tentacles!'

After that the twins were as good as goldfish. We sort of forgot about the Helpers Meeting though, and ended up playing **'Make Captain Tentacles Walk the Plank'**. So we still don't have any ideas for getting Help Points! I think Ozzie is a bit cross with me about the walking the plank thing, too.☹

Thought of the Day: Some days are Thinking Big days and some are Walking the Plank days.

39

FLOUNDERSDAY

When I went to get breakfast this morning, the prawnflake box was empty and Remy was hiding under the table with prawnflakes round his mouth.

'Remy!' I groaned. 'You're so greedy.'

Dad grinned. 'He needs a good workout. He should go to Zumba. Dance off that prawnflake belly!'

'That's silly, pets don't do . . .'

BLAM! A whopper of an idea whacked me on the nose.

'Dad, you're a genius!' I put Remy on his lead and whizzed round to Myrtle's.

'PET EXERCISING!' I burst out when she opened the door.

Myrtle looked confused. Then she said, 'Oh, like taking them for a swim?'

'Better. PET ZUMBA. I bet no one has ever thought of that!'

Myrtle said there might be a good reason why no one has thought of it, but I think

41

she sometimes has problems thinking **BIG**, because her brain is not as big as mine. She said taking pets for swims might be better. I said we could decide exactly what activities to do later, but right now we'd have to make a sign so people knew about us.

We set to work.

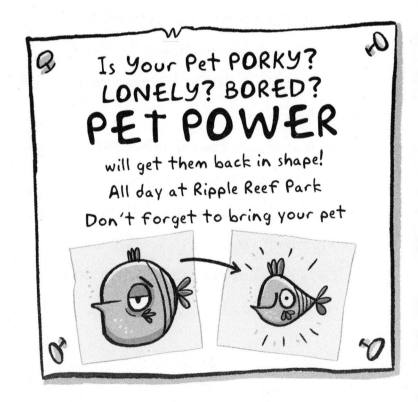

We both agreed that it was a **fintastic** sign.

We called for Ozzie and told him the plan. He didn't exactly look thrilled, but I said I was Shoal Leader, and eventually he said okay. We headed for the park, put the sign up on a rock, and settled down to wait.

No one came. After a while I started doing Zumba lunges to keep myself busy.

'Stretch – and – PUSH! Stretch – and – Oops!'

I lunged straight into a large grouper.

'Whoa!' he said, startled. He peered at the sign. 'What's all this, then?'

'Pet Power,' I said. 'It's keep fit for pets.'

I noticed a sleepy-looking sea snail trailing behind him on a lead.

'Your snail looks like he needs a bit of Pet Power,' I said. The grouper looked doubtful, but then handed me the lead.

'Well . . . all right then. Come along, Timmy . . .' Our first customer! 'Timmy will be literally **oozing** with power after his workout!' I promised.

The grouper wandered off while I took Timmy for a warm up swim. He kept falling asleep, and wanted to eat *everything*. It took me an hour to drag him once round the park. Then it was Zumba time.

I put Timmy in front of me. He instantly fell asleep.

'Get ready to ZUMBA,' I shouted. His eyes popped open.

I started prancing about.

'Wiggle, wiggle, wiggle! Shake your shell! Twist and bend! Zumba! Zumba!' I called to Timmy, leaping around encouragingly.

Timmy stared at me, mouth open.

'Lunge, Timmy, lunge!' I cried, lunging. Timmy let out a howl of fright and disappeared into his shell. No amount of knocking would

bring him out of it. He was still in there when
the grouper came back. He picked up Timmy
and peered into his shell.

'Well, he's oozing all right,' he said. 'But he doesn't look powerful. He looks dead.'

'He'll be fine,' I said, hoping it was true. 'He's just had a good workout!'

The grouper ticked off two Help Points on our card and trundled off, still peering into Timmy's shell.

'Two points – that's good,' said Ozzie.

I sighed. 'It's a start – but we need more! I know – we'll make some posters and put them up around town tomorrow.'

Thought of the Day: It takes more than one sea snail to win a Golden Woggle.

SALMONSDAY

I didn't sleep a **wink** last night thinking about
Help Points. This morning Myrtle and Ozzie
came round to make **posters**. Then we
headed into town, put the posters up, then
swam to the park. There was no one there, so
we settled down to wait.

I was tired after my sleepless night, and my
eyelids started drooping. To my surprise, the
Golden Woggle appeared and spoke to
me.

'I'm all yours Daaarcy,' it tinkled.

'Daaaaaarcy . . .'

'. . . DARCY!!!'

I woke up with a start. It wasn't the Golden Woggle, it was Myrtle yelling in my ear.

'Darcy! Customers!'

I nearly did a backflip in surprise. In front of our rock was a humungously long queue of sea creatures, each with a pet! One dogfish,

one catfish, one rabbitfish, one moray eel,
three sea slugs, four limpets, seventeen
sea snails and one giant clam. They were all
growling and snapping at each other.

It took a while, but we eventually got them quiet.

'Okay pets, let's Zumba!' I called.

It went wrong from the start. The limpets wouldn't lunge. The sea slugs squirted goo at each other. The dogfish **lunged** at the catfish, who chased the rabbitfish into the giant clam, which snapped shut. Ozzie had to squeeze inside the clam and tickle it to get the rabbitfish out. The eel gobbled up seven sea snails before anyone noticed, but he spat them out when I threatened to tell his owner.

When the owners came back to collect their gibbering, slightly chewed pets, Myrtle got them all to sign the Help Points card. As the last one left, she nudged me.

'Look – it's Miss Batfish.'

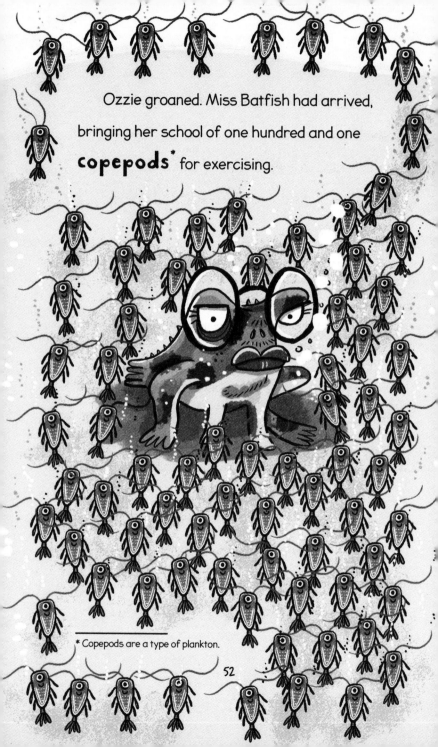

Ozzie groaned. Miss Batfish had arrived, bringing her school of one hundred and one **copepods*** for exercising.

* Copepods are a type of plankton.

52

'Colin is being dreadfully difficult today,'
she said, pointing into the crowd of copepods.
'You'll have to keep an eye on him.'

'Which one is Colin?' I asked, but she'd
ambled off already.

We put them into rows. Most stayed put,
but one in the back row kept swimming out of
line. Then it blew a loud raspberry. The other
copepods started giggling.

'Colin? Behave yourself,' I said sternly. The
copepod smirked, but stayed still.

'That's better.' I clapped my fins. 'Are you
ready to Zumba?'

'WHALE!' squeaked a tiny voice.

Every copepod vanished instantly. They
were so quick I didn't see them go. It took
Myrtle, Ozzie and I aaaages to tempt them

out of their hiding places and get them back into their lines. I spotted Colin in the back row.

'Coliiiin,' I said. He gazed at me innocently. 'Did you think there was a big scary whale?'

Colin nodded.

'There wasn't.'

Colin's eye swivelled from side to side.

'See? No whale.'

Colin grinned. He opened his mouth.

'WHAAAAAAALE!'

'THERE'S NO WHALE!' I yelled, a krillisecond too late. The copepods had already vanished.

When we had finally rounded them all up again, Myrtle said maybe we should stop Zumba lessons for today. 'We've got thirty Help Points already,' she added.

I nodded. 'Okay. We'd better count the copepods, though.'

Ozzie counted. It took a while. 'One hundred,' he finally declared.

I blinked. 'There should be a hundred and ONE!'

Myrtle counted. Then I did. Each time, the answer was the same. One copepod was missing.

I groaned. 'Colin!'

We searched and searched, and called and called, but we couldn't find Colin anywhere. With a feeling of **doom**, I saw Miss Batfish coming back.

I was going to tell her about Colin, but she went on and on about how nice we were to look after her precious babies, and I sort of forgot to mention him. When she'd gone, we searched again, but finally had to give up and go home.

I'm mega-worried now. I really hope Colin is okay. He might be a pain, but he's only little. I'll go have to go back tomorrow and have another look for him.

Thought of the Day: You can have too many pets.

SPONGEDAY

Early this morning the doorbell rang. Mum answered it, and I heard Miss Batfish's voice. My heart sank. I hid in my room, but a minute later Mum's head poked round the door.

'Darcy, one of Miss Batfish's copepods is missing. Do you know anything about that?'

I panicked. For a krillisecond I thought about just saying 'No.'

But I'm rubbish at lying. I burst into tears.

'I lost him!' I wailed. 'We searched everywhere, but we couldn't find him.'

Mum looked serious. 'Why didn't you say anything? Poor Miss Batfish is very upset.'

I sniffled. 'I was going to go back today and look for him.'

'Yes, you had better do that,' said Mum. 'I'll make Miss Batfish a cup of sea, and you go and look for Colin.'

I went to get Myrtle and Ozzie and we swam to the park. We looked under every rock and behind every clump of seaweed, but there was no sign of Colin.

'Triple fishsticks!' I cried. 'Now what can we do?'

Myrtle looked at me. 'What are dolphins really good at?' she said suddenly.

I sighed. 'Messing things up.'

'No, silly,' Myrtle said. 'I mean that thing you do to find things by clicking.'

'Echolocation*!' I gasped. 'Why didn't I think of that?!'

I started clicking.

CLICK CLICK CLICK.

I waited for an echo. Nothing.

Ozzie's tentacles drooped. 'He could be miles away by now.'

---

* Echolocation is something dolphins do to find food. We click to make sound waves that travel through water, bounce off an object, and come back to us as echoes. If we hear an echo, we know something is nearby, and we can find it quickly. Clever, huh?!

I tried again. **CLICK CLICK CLICK.**

After a second, I heard a faint echo.

CLICK CLICK CLICK. Just the right

sort of echo for . . .

'A copepod!' I shouted. 'It might be Colin!'

I started swimming towards the echo, clicking

like mad. The echo got stronger. It was coming

from off the reef, in the open sea. As I swam

towards it, I spotted a small dark shape in the

blue.

'Is that Colin?' asked Myrtle, from behind me. The shape got **bigger . . . and bigger . . . and bigger . . . and whale-shaped**. My heart sank.

It was Walter, the school whale.

'That echo must have been Walter,' I said, puzzled. 'That's weird. I was sure it was something much smaller . . .'

I spotted a shape bobbing around in front

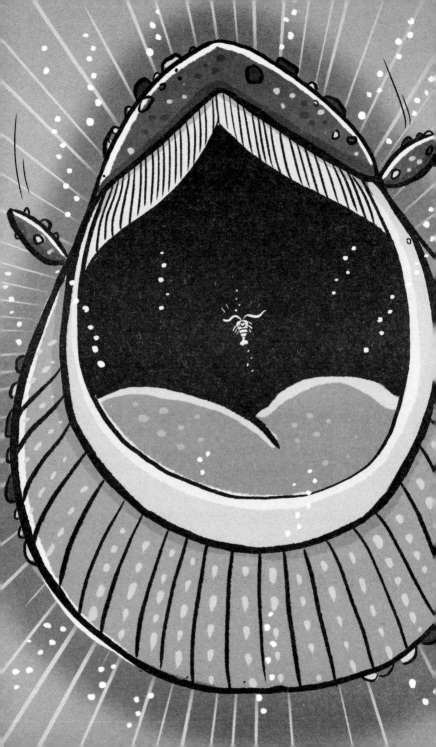

of Walter. The shape saw me and stuck its tongue out.

'Colin!' I shouted. Walter opened his huge mouth . . .

'WHALE!' I yelled at Colin.

Colin looked up, saw Walter and froze in terror. I flicked my tail as hard as I could and shot forward – just in time to shove Colin away to safety.

Walter looked a bit surprised, but not half as surprised as Colin. I put him back on his lead and took him home. He was very quiet all the way and didn't stick his tongue out once. Miss Batfish was so happy to see him that she gave us five Help Points. So now we have thirty-five Help Points – we must be in the lead!

Thought of the Day: If at first you don't succeed, try echolocation.

WEEK 2:
The Happy Abyss Retired Sharks' Home

MONKFISHDAY

When we got to Sea Trouts this evening,
Brown Trout took everyone's Help Points
cards, and wrote how many points each Shoal
had earned on a chart on the wall. Everyone
crowded round to look.

HELP POINTS CHART	
Anchovies:	31
Blennies:	30
Guppies:	37
Minnows:	35

I couldn't believe my eyes!

'Flippering fishsticks!' I muttered to Ozzie and Myrtle. 'Guppies are winning. We need to help like we've never helped before if we want to win that Golden Woggle!'

Myrtle said second place was pretty good. Then Ozzie said he didn't mind not winning if it meant we could stop exercising crazy pets. I told him he wasn't being a **team player**. Then he got all grumpy and Myrtle told me not to be mean to Ozzie. I opened my mouth to speak but then Brown Trout called for silence.

'You're all doing amazingly well, Sea Trouts! Now, this week I've got a special challenge for you. Some community organisations have written to me saying they need helpers, so I'm going to ask each Shoal to choose a job . . .'

Myrtle started whispering again. 'Darcy, you *have* been a bit bossy lately.'

'Well, I am Shoal Leader,' I whispered back.

'So?'

'So I have to tell you what to do.'

'No you don't.'

'I DO,' I said. It came out louder than I meant it to.

'Excellent – thank you Darcy!' Brown Trout was looking at me. 'Darcy has just volunteered Minnows to help out at the **Happy Abyss Retired Sharks' Home**.'

My mouth fell open. 'W-what? Hang on! I – I didn't mean –'

But Brown Trout didn't hear. 'Now who's up for litter picking in the park? Guppies! Wonderful . . .'

Brown Trout finished giving out the help

tasks, then it was snack time.

'Oh, why couldn't we get the litter-picking

job,' moaned Ozzie. 'I've never been a big fan

of sharks. It's those little spooky eyes . . . and

the fact that they eat us . . .'

'They won't eat us,' I said. A deep voice in

my ear made me jump.

'Be CAREFUL at Happy Abyss, Daaaaarcy.'

It was that flat-faced **nitwit**, Reggie Ray.

He leaned over. 'My cousin's best friend's sister went there one day and was NEVER SEEN AGAIN.'

He swam off, laughing evilly.

'Well, good luck litter picking!' I shouted after him. 'I've heard there's some dangerous – um – sea slugs in the park!'

Ha. That told him. And you know what? I'm fine with sharks.

Totally. Fine. With. Sharks.

Thought for the Day: Saying 'I do' can get you in a heap of trouble.

TUNASDAY

Myrtle and Ozzie picked me up early. Ozzie was a sickly grey colour, and Myrtle hardly said a word. Although I was nervous too, as Shoal Leader I couldn't show it. I tried to cheer them up.

'Guys . . . Remy was funny this morning. He poked his head in a shell and guess what – he got stuck! He was swimming round and round with the shell on his head . . . Ozzie?'

Ozzie had turned a nasty shade of green. He pointed at a sign just ahead.

HAPPY ABYSS RETIRED SHARKS' HOME

An arrow pointed down into a deep, not-very-happy-looking abyss. Myrtle squeaked and disappeared into her shell.

'We'll be fine,' I said. 'Just . . . stick together, okay?'

They looked at each other and gulped. 'Okay.'

As we swam into the depths, a row of caves appeared in the gloom. Something suddenly shot out of one, making me jump. It was a lobster, who started talking at top speed.

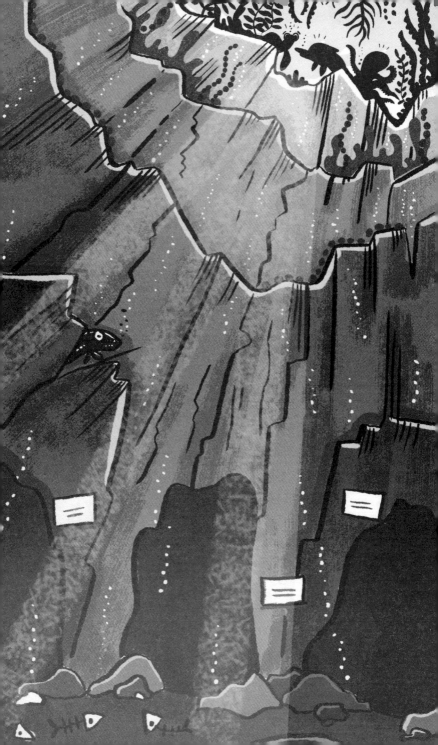

'Are you my helpers? I'm Lobelia, the manager. We've got three sharks living here, so that's one shark each. Now, please keep the noise down at all times. The sharks need peace and quiet . . .'

She pointed at some signs pinned to the abyss wall.

74

NO ARGUING

NO LAUGHING

NO MUSIC

NO SHOUTING

IF YOU MUST MOVE, DO IT QUIETLY

'They must be very frail,' said Myrtle, hopefully.

Lobelia snorted. 'It's nothing to do with being frail. Over-excitement makes sharks **HUNGRY**. So keep the noise down unless you want to be on the menu. Now, off you pop and introduce yourselves. *Quietly.*'

Lobelia shot back into her cave in a swirl of mud.

Ozzie was quivering. 'We're DOOMED.'

'Shhh,' I said. 'We have to be quiet.'

'We're doomed,' I heard him whisper as

75

we swam along the rockface. There were three caves in it, each with a sign above the entrance.

| Miss Wilma Wobbegong | Major Monty Mako | Madame Blanche Legrand |

'I'm Shoal Leader so I'll choose,' I said. 'I'll take Madame Legrand.' I thought she sounded nice. 'Ozzie, you take Major Mako, which leaves Myrtle with Miss Wobble-along.'

Ozzie looked like he was about to argue, so I pointed to the NO ARGUING sign.

He glared. 'Fine. But if I get eaten it's your fault.'

'They won't be hungry this soon after

breakfast,' I said, hoping this was true.

Steeling myself, I swam bravely forward into Madame Legrand's cave.

I nearly swam un-bravely out again.

Glaring at me from the darkness was a humungous **GREAT WHITE SHARK!**

'Who are YOU?' she snapped.

When she opened her mouth, I realised she didn't have a single tooth in it.

'I'm Darcy, your new helper,' I said, dizzy with relief.

Madame Legrand stared at me till I started to feel a bit twitchy.

'Well!' she barked, making me jump. She pointed to a table. 'Help me put my teeth in, then!'

My relief drained away. The most ginormous-est set of false teeth was grinning  at me from a **whale-sized** glass. They gleamed evilly, and looked horribly sharp.

'Get a move on,'

said Madame Legrand, licking her gums.

Feeling the shark's beady eyes on me, I heaved the teeth out of the glass and inched towards her, holding them VERY carefully ... closer ... closer ... I stopped in front of her open, cavernous mouth, heart pounding. Any moment she could pounce forward and swallow me whole ...

I reached up and tried to push the teeth into her gums. At first they wouldn't go in, and for one horrible moment I had to put my head right inside her mouth. **CLICK!** The teeth slid into place. I shot out backwards as fast as I could, as – **CLANG!** – the jaws clamped shut.

She gave me a toothy grin. 'What's the matter? I'm not going to BITE you. Now clean my gills!'

The rest of the day was a nightmare. It was all 'Do this, do that!' I wouldn't have minded – except everything I did was wrong.

On the bright side, she didn't eat me.

On the way home, I asked Ozzie and Myrtle how their sharks had been, and they said they were nice. NICE?! I picked

Madame Legrand because I thought SHE

sounded nice! ☹

Thought of the Day: Sharks always have

teeth.

WHALESDAY

Myrtle and Ozzie were so chirpy on the way to Happy Abyss this morning. They chatted away about Major Mako and Miss Wobbegong like they were old friends. Ozzie noticed I wasn't joining in and asked me what was wrong.

'Everything!' I said. 'Madame Legrand was grumpy and mean, and said I hadn't done anything right.'

'Miss Wobbegong does seaweed arranging,' Myrtle said. 'Why don't you take Madame Legrand some pretty seaweed?

It might cheer her up.'

I didn't think Madame Legrand was the
type to be cheered up by seaweed, but I picked
a few bits anyway. When we arrived, I swam to
her cave.

'Hello?' I called.

There was a grunt from inside. I thought
that must mean 'Come in', so I did. The old
shark was lying on a sofa, with sea cucumbers
on her eyes. I've seen Aunt Ditzy do that –

it's some sort of beauty treatment. Madame Legrand pulled the sea cucumbers off and sat up. The beauty treatment hadn't worked that well.

She scowled at me. 'Who are you?'

Not a good start. 'I'm Darcy – remember? Your helper.'

'Oh yes. The dolphin.' She heaved her humungous self off the sofa and slunk towards me, a cunning look on her face. 'I like dolphins,' she said.

'Thanks!' I said, surprised.

'FOR BREAKFAST!' She opened her mouth, and with one big thrash of her tail, she shot towards me.

'AAAAAAAAAAAAARGH!' I screamed, dropped the seaweed and fled out of the cave,

crashing straight into Lobelia who was just outside.

'The rules clearly state NO shouting!' she exclaimed.

'Madame Legrand said she was going to eat me,' I panted.

'Ah, she's probably tetchy because she hasn't had breakfast,' said Lobelia, waving a claw. 'Once she's eaten something she'll be fine.'

Hmm. Well, she was fine – for a bit. But at lunchtime she tried to take a nibble out of my tail, saying it looked like a tuna sandwich. After lunch she made me clean her teeth (while they were still in her mouth), read the whole of the *Daily Echo* (including the adverts) and dust the photos on her continental shelf. One of the photos was of a shark posing dramatically on

a stage.

'Careful with that!' she said, grabbing it

off me.

'Is that you?' I asked, curiously.

'Yes,' she said. 'I used to be in theatre. That

was a performance of *Beauty and the Beast*.'

I was impressed, and looked at the picture again. 'You made a good Beast . . .'

'I WAS BEAUTY!!!'

After that she went into a **massive** sulk and refused to say goodbye when I left.

'There must be something that would cheer her up,' Ozzie said on the way home. Right now I think the only thing that would cheer her up is if I was served to her in a sandwich!

Thought of the Day: When you swim with sharks, try not to look like a tuna sandwich.

TURTLESDAY

I thought about what Ozzie had said about
cheering Madame Legrand up, and it gave me
a **Good Idea**. So this morning I rootled
around in the toy cave and found some
board games: Prawntrap, Crabsticks and my
favourite – Eels and Ladders, with real eels.
Remy tried to help by getting in the way and
nibbling the boxes. I thought about taking him
to Happy Abyss with me, but Lobelia would
have a fit.

Ozzie said we could get all the sharks to

play the games and have a tournament. But Lobelia wasn't sure.

'I keep the sharks away from each other,' she said. 'They end up arguing, and . . .' She made a slicing movement with her pincer. Just then, Myrtle's head popped round the door.

'Miss Wobbegong says we can play the tournament in her cave!' she said.

Lobelia agreed in the end. 'Just make sure they don't start arguing!' She wagged her claw at me.

Miss Wobbegong's cave was cosy, with fancy seaweed arrangements everywhere. Major Mako and Madame Legrand arrived just as I had set the board up.

'Let battle commence!' roared Major Mako, so loudly that Miss Wobbegong shot under the table in fright.

'Calm yourself, Major,' said Madame

Legrand coldly. 'You're not in the navy now.'

I rolled the dice quickly before they could start squabbling. For a while everything went swimmingly, although Madame Legrand went into a sulk whenever she landed on an eel. I was neck and neck with Madame Legrand, and we both needed a six to win. Throwing a four would land on a very long eel. It was Madame Legrand's turn.

'Throw a four, throw a four,' I said (in my head of course).

Madame Legrand threw a four.

'Six – I win!' she cried, snatching the dice up and moving her counter to the last square.

What?! 'That was a four!' I exclaimed. 'You have to go down that eel.'

Myrtle nudged me, hard. 'Darcy . . .'

Madame Legrand glared. 'It was a six.'

I felt **crossness** building up in my tummy.

'It was a four,' I said.

'Darcy!' Ozzie was trying to put a tentacle

over my mouth. I pulled it off.

'Cheat!' I cried.

Madame Legrand puffed up like an angry pufferfish.

'NEVER in my LIFE have I, Blanche Legrand, respectable denizen of the deep, been accused of CHEATING!'

'Oh, don't be a drama queen, Blanche,' said Major Mako. 'You're not in the theatre now.'

Oops. Wrong thing to say. Madame Legrand went **purple**. She picked up the board and threw it, eels and all, at Major Mako. Major Mako ducked. The board whizzed over his head and hit one of Miss Wobbegong's seaweed arrangements, which flopped right onto Miss Wobbegong's head. She howled and started swimming in panicked circles.

The confused eels tried to bite anything
that moved. One bit Madame Legrand's tail.
Madame Legrand thought Major Mako had

bitten her, and chased him round the cave. Ozzie, Myrtle and I managed to escape, and fled round a corner to wait for things to calm down.

After a bit, we saw Madame Legrand come out of Miss Wobbegong's cave and swim huffily back to her own cave, and a few minutes later, Major Mako came out too. We crept back in to try and help Miss Wobbegong clean up the mess, but then Lobelia appeared and we had to explain what happened. She was NOT a happy lobster.

Somehow I don't think we'll get many Help Points today. ☹

Thought of the Day: Never play Eels and Ladders with a shark (they cheat).

FLOUNDERSDAY

I couldn't face going to Happy Abyss after yesterday, so this morning I decided to have a toothache. I stuffed seaweed in my cheeks to make my mouth look swollen.

'I inky oomphy ooth ache,' I said to Mum.
(It's hard talking with a mouth full of seaweed.)
But she wasn't listening. She was trying to
wrestle Diddy into his buggy.

'Diddy, sit still! Darcy, I'm taking Diddy for
a check-up at the doctor so you'll have to take
Remy with you to Happy Abyss today.'

'Mmmf–' I spat my seaweed out. 'Mum . . .'

But she was halfway out the door. 'Bye,
sweetiefins!'

Remy looked at me, panting. I sighed.

'Looks like you're coming with me then,
Remy. But we'll have to hide you from Lobelia.' I
got my rucksack and put Remy in it.

'Stay still. And don't make any noise.'

When we got there, Lobelia was putting
another sign up. **NO BOARD GAMES**.

I snuck past her and into Madam Legrand's cave, feeling Remy wriggling in my rucksack.

'My teeth!' snapped Madame Legrand, as soon as she saw me.

'Good morning,' I said in a cheery, 'everything's fine' sort of voice. I put the rucksack with Remy in by the door and went to get her teeth. But before I could, she let out a startled cry.

'What in Neptune's name is THAT?'

I looked round. The rucksack was hopping around in a very **unrucksacklike** way.

'Remy!' I grabbed the bag, but I grabbed too hard. It burst open and Remy popped out. He shot across to Madame Legrand, and attached himself to her nose.

Madame Legrand squawked. She pulled Remy off and held him up, wriggling frantically.

'Is it lunch?' she asked, astonished.

I squeaked. 'NO! It's Remy, my pet remora. I'm sorry . . . Mum was going out, and –'

Remy licked Madame Legrand's nose.

'Stop it, Remy!' I exclaimed. But then Madame Legrand did something surprising.

She laughed!

'What a funny little fellow! Does ickle fishy-wishy want a biccie-wiccie?'

'So . . . you're not cross with me?' I asked, hopefully.

Madame Legrand didn't hear. She was as **gooey** as a sea slug over Remy! He seemed to like her too, I think because she gave him a ton of biccie-wiccies. She even gave me a packet to take home. ☺

When we had to leave, Remy didn't want to go back in the rucksack. In the end, we got him in using a biccie-wiccie as bait. Lobelia gave me a very odd look when I went past her office leaving a trail of crumbs behind me. ☺

Ozzie and Myrtle were very quiet on the way home. They said their sharks had been down in the dumps all day about the board game, and were refusing to come out of their caves.

Later at home Remy jumped up and licked my nose. Suddenly I felt happier . . . weird, because Madame Legrand went all funny went Remy licked her nose. Remy must have magic powers or something . . .

DING! I suddenly had another one of my famous **brainwaves**! I have got the most crabulously cunning plan to get those sharks

out of their grumps – *and* win us a heap of

Help Points!

Thought of the Day: Even the toughest old

shark has a soft spot.

SALMONSDAY

This morning I put my plan into action. I managed to get Remy back in the rucksack using one of the biccies Madame Legrand gave me. Then I swam to Ozzie's. His mum opened the door.

'Oh, it's you, Darcy,' she said. 'I thought it was the postman.' She whispered in my ear, 'It's Ozzie's birthday next Spongeday and we're waiting for his present! Don't say anything to him though . . . oh there you are, Ozzie.'

She vanished back into the shipwreck as Ozzie came out.

'Was Mum talking about my birthday present again?' He grinned. 'She thinks I don't know. Hey – there's something moving in your bag, Darcy!'

I told him my cunning plan for cheering up the sharks.

'Madame Legrand **LOVED** Remy,' I said. 'No one can be miserable for long with a pet. So I thought you could take Cuke to meet Major Mako, and Myrtle could take Squishy to meet Miss Wobbegong. I bet you five hundred Jiggling Jellies that will cheer them all up!'

Ozzie said no at first, because of Lobelia. But I reminded him that I was Shoal Leader, and eventually he said okay. We got Cuke into the rucksack using biccies as bait, then set off to Myrtle's. Squishy, Myrtle's vampire squid, was trickier and kept shooting off backwards in a cloud of ink, but we did it in the end (with the help of more biccies).

Actually we needn't have worried. A sign was hanging on Lobelia's office door saying **GONE SHOPPING**.

'Perfect!' I said, relieved.

Ozzie and Myrtle took Cuke and Squishy out of the rucksack and went off to see their sharks. I went into Madame Legrand's cave.

She was super-happy to see Remy! She'd even made him a name-tag out of one of her old teeth.

I was fixing it to his collar when Ozzie's head poked round the door.

'You have to see this,' he said, a big grin on his face. I followed him out curiously, with Madame Legrand just behind me.

Major Mako and Miss Wobbegong were leading Cuke and Squishy round and round the abyss floor by their leads, beaming like sunfish.

'That's the spirit, Cuke my lad! Up two three four . . .' barked Major Mako. As they came past Madame Legrand's cave, he called out to her.

'Come and join us, Blanche,' he called. 'Nothing like a bracing march to get the juices flowing!'

Before I knew it, Madame Legrand and

Remy had joined in the pet parade, and it wasn't long before they were all chattering away like old buddies. Myrtle, Ozzie and I grinned at each other. This was even better than I'd hoped for. Pets really do have magic powers, I thought ...

But then I heard a shriek.

'WHAT IN THE SEA IS GOING ON?!'

Lobelia was back from shopping. She had a look on her face as if she'd seen a herd of zombie crabs side-stepping towards her.

'They're just, um, taking our pets for a swim,' I said, trying to smile reassuringly.

'PETS?!' Her antennae started twitching so fast I thought they'd fly off. 'You can't bring PETS to a retired shark's home! There will be over-excitement! Arguments! **Chaos and devastation** –'

'Utter PIFFLE!' Madame Legrand boomed.

All three sharks were swimming towards us. Lobelia started backing away.

'All of you – please! Pets are far too exciting for you. Think of your hearts!'

'We like the pets,' said Major Mako, patting Cuke.

Miss Wobbegong smiled fondly at Squishy. 'We are thinking of our hearts.'

'I haven't had so much fun in YEARS!' boomed Madame Legrand, giving Remy a biccie-wiccie.

'On the left, quick march!' called Major Mako. And with that the three old sharks swam off, with Squishy, Cuke and Remy in tow. A thud behind me made me look round.

Lobelia had fainted.

Thought of the Day: A little over-excitement won't do you any harm (except if you're a lobster, maybe).

SPONGEDAY

That wasn't the end of the story, though. We'd thought everything had gone brilliantly, but when Lobelia came out of her faint she gave us a long telling off.

Then she put up two new signs:

There was nothing we could do except take the pets home. When I told Mum and Dad what happened, Dad said, 'Well, you can't win 'em all.'

'We didn't even get any Help Points,' I said – and then I remembered. Not only had Lobelia not given us any Help Points, she still had our Help Points card. However cross she was, she'd have to give the card back!

So I phoned Ozzie and Myrtle this morning and they reluctantly agreed to come to Happy Abyss with me, as long as I did all the talking.

'Fine,' I said. But I couldn't help feeling nervous as we swam there. Would Lobelia be cross still? Would she –

'Look!' squeaked Myrtle, pointing.

I looked. Just ahead, three sharks were swimming towards us. Madame Legrand was in front with a very frilly sea slug on a lead. Major Mako had a little pink sea snail and Miss

Wobbegong had a beefy-looking moray eel.

Astonished, we swam to meet them.

'Darcy, meet Frou Frou,' said Madame

Legrand, giving her slug an adoring look.

'Hello Frou Frou,' I said. 'But . . . what about

Lobelia?'

'What about me?' Lobelia's twitching

antennae appeared round the side of Madame

Legrand. I gulped and started talking quickly.

'Um, Lobelia, we're **really REALLY**

sorry about bringing the pets and causing too

much excitement and stuff but we really want

. . . in fact, we need . . .'

'To be congratulated!' said Lobelia.

I gaped. 'Congratu– what?'

'Congratulated! You worked miracles

yesterday. I've never seen the sharks so cheerful. So I had a think about it, and this morning we went to Pollock's Pet Shop. I even got a pet myself . . .'

From behind Lobelia peeked a rainbow-coloured shrimp.

'This is Brucie,' said Lobelia, proudly. 'He's a mantis shrimp. Cute, isn't he?'

Ozzie turned a terrified purple and green and shot behind me.

'Oh yes – very, um . . . cute.' I wondered if Lobelia knew that mantis shrimps can knock you out with one blow of their claw. But seeing her and the sharks so happy gave me a warm, glowy feeling. Ozzie and Myrtle looked all **glowy**, too.

'Well, we'd better go,' I said. We said our goodbyes and started to swim off.

'Haven't you forgotten something?' Lobelia called. I looked back. She was waving something.

'The Help Points card!' exclaimed Myrtle.

I can't believe I nearly forgot that! I swam

119

back and took the card from Lobelia. As she and the sharks swam off into the blue, I looked at the card.

'Thirty Help Points!' I exclaimed.

Ozzie and Myrtle gasped. 'Wow!'

I grabbed both of them and we did a little victory dance.

'THANK YOU, LOBELIA! THANK YOU, SHARKS!'

Thought of the Day: The world is your lobster!

WEEK 3:
The Best Party Ever!

MONKFISHDAY

Only one more week of helping before we find
out who wins the **Golden Woggle**! This
evening Brown Trout added up all the points
again, and wrote them on the chart:

```
HELP POINTS CHART
Anchovies:   60
Blennies:    57
Guppies:     65
Minnows:     65
```

We were neck and neck with Guppies! Grrr.

How were they getting so many points? I saw

Reggie looking at me smugly. He saw me too,
and stuck his tongue out. I stuck mine out back.

'Darcy!' Brown Trout was scowling at me
disapprovingly. 'Sea Trouts, to your Shoals!'

There was a flurry as everyone zipped to
their Shoals.

'Well done everyone for all your excellent helping last week. Now, today I want you to think about your **FRIENDS**. We have to be nice to our friends and help them whenever we can. So this week our special Lend a Fin task will be to **Help Our Friends**.'

At the end of Sea Trouts, I asked Myrtle if she had any ideas about the new task.

'Well, you're my friend,' Myrtle said. 'What do you want me to help you with?'

'I dunno.' I thought for a moment. 'Help me get the Golden Woggle!'

She laughed. 'You're obsessed with that thing.'

'Am not!' I turned to Ozzie. 'What about you, Ozzie? Do you want help with something – Ozzie! Are you even listening?'

Ozzie blinked. 'What? Sorry . . .'

'It's Ozzie's birthday on Spongeday,' Myrtle said. 'Bet you were thinking about that, weren't you, Ozzie?'

'Well . . .'

'Flippering fishsticks,' I exclaimed, nearly turning a backflip in surprise. 'I almost forgot about your birthday! Are you having a party? Am I invited?'

Ozzie turned pinky-mauve. 'Yes I am having a party, and of course you're invited –'

I was super – sorry, **MEGA** – excited!

'OMG, a party!'

I squeaked. (I love parties more than I love Jiggling Jellies!) 'Oh I can't wait till Spongeday . . . is it fancy dress?'

Ozzie looked nervously at me. 'It's only a small party. Five or six friends, and a cake . . .'

'Cake!' (I LOVE CAKE TOO!) 'What sort of cake?'

'Fishcake,' said Ozzie.

'Why don't I make it?' I said.

'It's okay, Mum likes making cakes. She makes the best fishcake ever.'

Hmmf. I bet my cakes are better than Ozzie's mum's!

But OMG. A party. A **PARTY**!

Thought of the Day: PARTY PARTY PARTY PARTY PARTY!

TUNASDAY

After breakfast I zoomed round to Myrtle's.

'Shall we get started then?' I said.

Myrtle looked puzzled. 'Started on what?'

'Planning Ozzie's party, of course!'

Myrtle looked thoughtful. 'Well, I suppose –'

'We can make it fancy dress, and do party food. And music . . . now, who to invite? Our class. And all the other classes. Oh, and the Sea Trouts. We'll ask the guests to give us a Help Point each –'

'Ozzie said he wanted a small party,'

Myrtle interrupted. 'He's quite shy. We should ask him first.'

'I'm Shoal Leader –' I began. But Myrtle dragged me round to Ozzie's.

Ozzie said there wasn't much to help with. Just some food and a few decorations. But I had to try and convince him to let us help.

'Can't I at least plan some party games?' I begged. 'Please . . . pretty please . . .'

Ozzie **ummed** and **ahhed**, and finally gave in.

'Okay. You and Myrtle can help me plan the party. But it's my party, so I can say yes or no to things.'

Yes yes yes!

'It's a deal,' I said, shaking Ozzie's tentacle.

Ozzie got a piece of paper and a pen and

we set to work.

'Now let's think up some games,' I said when we'd finished, but just then Ozzie's mum came out and said Ozzie had to go to his gran's.

Ozzie's Party

Small party (five or six friends)
Food
A few decorations
Cake (Fishcake)
3 x Games

I tucked the **Party Plan** under my fin.
'I'll have a look at it tonight and see if there's anything we missed.'

I swam home through the park, whistling happily. Ozzie's party was going to be fab, we were going to earn lots of Help Points, I was thinking of some fun games . . .

'HEY, DARCY!'

Fishsticks! It was Reggie Ray, the Guppies leader. He hovered annoyingly over my head, grinning.

'What are Minnows doing for the last helping challenge then?'

I stuffed the Party Plan further under my fin so Reggie wouldn't see it.

'I'm not telling you!'

Reggie grinned. 'Well, I'd give up now if

I were you. We're going to win. We're
helping some friends set up a big finball
tournament!'

My mouth fell open. *A finball tournament?*
Reggie laughed at my face.

'So whatever you're doing isn't as good as
that, then?' he said.

A bubble of crossness in my brain suddenly went **POP!**

'Actually,' I said. 'We're planning a **BIG** party for Ozzie. The **BIGGEST** party you can imagine. There'll be music, and dancing, and, um . . .'

A poster on the park fence caught my eye.

'. . . a jellyfish lightshow!' I said triumphantly.

It was Reggie's turn to look stunned. 'Sounds rubbish,' he muttered, before flapping off out of the park.

I stormed home and stuck the Party Plan to my wall. I got a big pen out and set to work.

Jellyfish
Lightshow

The
Sparkling
Sea Gooseberries
**World Famous
Lightshow!**

Now **THAT'S** what I call a party! It will beat Reggie's finball tournament hands down!

Thought of the Day: Always plan for LOTS of cake.

WHALESDAY

This morning I showed Mum, Dad and Diddy
the Party Plan.

Dad whistled. 'That'll be quite a party.'

'Where will you get penguins?' Mum asked.
'You'll have to go to Antarctica!'

'Oh yeah.' I crossed that one out. Dad said
I would have to **delegate**.

'Delly-what?'

'Delegate. Give some jobs to other people.'

'Oh. Good idea! You can do some if you
like . . .'

Dad suddenly shot off in a rush, saying he had to see a man about a cod. I have no idea what he meant. Dad is so weird sometimes.

I swam to Myrtle's with the new Party Plan.

'Finally! I thought you weren't coming,' she said. 'Let's have a look at the plan, then.'

I spread it out on the seabed. Myrtle's eyes nearly popped out.

'A hundred invitations? Ozzie said five . . . and what's all this other stuff? Famous band? Jellyfish lightshow? Ozzie said he just wanted a cake and a few games . . .'

'He changed his mind,' I said quickly. Myrtle gave me a suspicious look.

'Really? He wants a big party now?'

'Yes. Come on, we need to start doing the invites.'

Myrtle got some paper and I started writing invitations. But after writing ten, my fin started to ache. I remembered what Dad said about delly-grating or something. Myrtle's twin brothers, Tyler and Trent, were hanging around being annoying, so I decided to give them a job.

'I'll give you a Jiggling Jelly for every invitation you write,' I said. 'And another if you can post them all, too.'

They were pretty happy to help, after that!
Myrtle looked at the plan again.

'Where are we going to find a jellyfish
lightshow?' she said.

That was easy. 'There's a poster in the
park for one. Let's go and have a look.'

We swam to the park and found the poster.

'The Sparkling Sea Gooseberries World
Famous Lightshow!' read Myrtle. 'Appearing
for one week only at Ripple Reef Theatre.' She
shook her head. 'World Famous! They'll never
come.'

'Yes they will! We just have to persuade
them,' I said. 'It's all about **Positive Mental
Attitude**, Myrtle. Look how I persuaded the
twins to write the invitations for us!'

Jellyfish Lightshow
The Sparkling Sea Gooseberries
World Famous Lightshow!

Myrtle said she didn't think **World Famous** people would be persuaded with Jiggling Jellies. She has a point. I never get why grown-ups think Jiggling Jellies are **EVIL** when they are totally scrummy-licious!

That evening my Aunt Ditzy came round for dinner and I told her about the Sparkling Sea Gooseberries. And – OMG – she actually KNOWS one of them – they used to go to dance classes together!

'I didn't know they were in town,' she said. 'I must invite Gabriella over for a cup of sea.'

'Aunt Ditzy,' I said, an **Idea** bubbling up in my brain. 'Why don't you invite her – and all her Sea Gooseberry friends – to Ozzie's birthday party on Spongeday?'

Aunt Ditzy said she hadn't realised she was invited to the party, but it sounded marvellous and of course she would love to come.

'There's no harm in asking Gabriella, I suppose,' she said. 'The theatre always has rehearsals in the mornings, so if we go early we should catch them.'

Thought of the Day: Aunts are sometimes extremely useful things!

TURTLESDAY

When Aunt Ditzy and I got to the theatre the ladyfish in the ticket office said there was a rehearsal going on, but we could watch from the back. We crept in, to find the Gooseberries were just finishing up in an explosion of multi-coloured lights*. 'Wow, they're amazing,' I whispered. I felt a twinge of nerves about asking them to the party. Aunt Ditzy must have sensed how I was feeling.

'Leave it to me,' she said. As the lights

---

* Sea Gooseberries are sort of like little jellyfish, with rows of coloured lights along their bodies. When they flash all together they look like a firework display.

faded and the Gooseberries started to float

off the stage, she sailed to the front. I quickly

followed.

'Gabriella!' she called up. 'Remember me?'

A pretty Gooseberry turned and floated

down.

'Goodness gracious!' she tinkled. 'Ditzy

Dolphin! You haven't changed one little bit! And

who's this?'

She was looking at me.

'My niece, Darcy.' Aunt Ditzy nudged me. 'Say hello, dear!'

'Hello,' I said, then felt shy and hid behind Aunt Ditzy. She and Gabriella chattered away and I was starting to think they'd forgotten I was there, when suddenly Aunt Ditzy turned to me.

'I almost forgot!' she said. 'Darcy is organising a birthday party for a friend on Spongeday and we wondered if you and the Gooseberries might like to come along and do a display?'

'Sounds lovely,' Gabriella said. 'Will there be cake?'

'Oh yes,' I said, forgetting to be shy. 'And Jiggling Jellies . . .'

Gabriella smiled. 'My favourite!' she said. 'I'd love to come. And I'll try and get some of the others to come too, to do a little show for your friend.'

'THANK YOU, THANK YOU!' I cried. I was so excited I could barely scribble down the address for her. As we left the theatre I let out a scream that made all the sea anemones on Aunt Ditzy's hat retract their tentacles in fright.

'OMG! THE SPARKLING SEA GOOSEBERRIES ARE COMING TO OUR PARTY!' I squeaked. 'I have to tell Myrtle right away!'

Myrtle was impressed (particularly by the fact that **World Famous People** like Jiggling Jellies).

'How about the music?' she asked.

'I've got an idea for that, too.' I paused, dramatically. 'The Deepsea Divas!'

Myrtle stared. '*The* Deepsea Divas? But they're even more famous than the Sparkling Sea Gooseberries! Darcy, sometimes I think you live in a dream world.'

That reminded me of one of the **Inspiring Thoughts** from my mum's book.

'If you can dream it, you can do it,' I declared.

Myrtle giggled. 'Last night I dreamed I turned into a giant sea anemone.'

'Well, you never know,' I said.

Thought of the Day: You will never know if you can turn into a giant sea anemone or not unless you try.

FLOUNDERSDAY

Mum and Dad think I am being a bit **over-optimistic** about the Deepsea Divas, but they let me go on the computer to find their website. There was a sea-mail address on it so I wrote asking if they could play at Ozzie's party. I waited for ages but they didn't reply. Dad said I should have a **Plan B**.

'What's a Plan B?' I asked.

He said that the Deepsea Divas were Plan A, but I should have another plan, Plan B, just in case they couldn't make it.

'Oh, yeah. Good idea.'

I decided to think about that later because today Myrtle and I were making our fancy-dress costumes. Myrtle couldn't decide what to go as.

'I know – you can be a sea anemone,' I said. 'Like in your dream!'

I got some glue from Dad's toolbox and some seaweed. Myrtle looked worried when she saw the glue.

'I think maybe I'll be a superhero–'

'Loads of people will be superheroes,' I said. 'Be a super sea anemone. Oh, that's funny – look, this glue is called superglue!'

Before she could argue, I started gluing seaweed onto her shell. When I had finished, Myrtle went to look in the mirror. She made a face.

'I don't look much like a sea anemone.'

She was right. She looked like a turtle with seaweed stuck to her.

'If you pull your head in you could be a seaweed arrangement,' I suggested.

'I don't want to be a seaweed arrangement!' Myrtle looked like she might cry, so I quickly changed the subject.

'What can I go as?' I looked around. I spotted Mum's mop in a corner. 'I know – I'll go as a **narwhal!**[*]'

I pulled the handle off the mop, stuck it to my nose and looked in the mirror.

'Hmmm. I don't look anything like a narwhal,' I said. 'I know, let's go as superheroes.'

---

[*] A narwhal is a small whale that basically looks like it has a mop handle stuck to its nose.

I tried to pull the mop handle off. To my horror it was stuck fast.

'Help!' I squeaked to Myrtle. She started pulling. 'Ow! Ooh! Stop!' I squeaked.

'It won't come off,' she panted. Then I tried to get the seaweed off her shell, but that was stuck too. There was only one thing to do.

Panic.

'I AM GOING TO HAVE A MOP HANDLE STUCK TO MY NOSE FOR THE REST OF MY LIFE!!!!'

Mum burst into the room. When she saw the superglue, she **totally** flippered out and said we would have to go to the doctor's to have it removed. Doctor Dab told us off too, and said he'd never seen anything like it in all his years of doctoring, and blah blah blah, but he got most of it off in the end.

I do still have a bit of superglue on my nose. I could go as Super-Dolphin, I suppose. Myrtle said she is going as herself.

Thought of the Day: Never stick things to your nose with superglue.

SALMONSDAY

Dad checked his sea-mail this morning, but the
Deepsea Divas still hadn't replied. I remembered
I was supposed to be making a Plan B – but
there wasn't time to think about that now. We
still had to get the party food – and make a
humungous **cake**! I decided I would definitely
delly-grate some jobs today.

I delly-grated the shopping to Mum, then
Myrtle arrived to help with the cake and I found
Mum's recipe book. Remy has eaten chunks out
of it, so I couldn't read some of the ingredients.

'Ten jealous sea squirts?' I asked, pointing. 'How can you tell if they're jealous?'

'Jellied, I think,' said Myrtle.

We found as many ingredients as we could, then I looked at the instructions.

'This looks tricky,' I said. 'Why don't we just throw everything in a bowl and mix it up?'

We did that.

Myrtle licked the spoon. 'It tastes weird. And what's happening to the sea squirts?'

They had puffed up to twice their normal size.

'I think that's normal. Mum says cakes

have to rise, or something.'

We had just put the cake in the oven when Mum came back from shopping. I rummaged through the bags. But what was this? Low-fat seaweed rolls? 100% organic algae bars? Freshly squeezed kelp juice?! I emptied the bags in a **panic**.

'Mum! You picked up someone else's shopping,' I cried. 'The party food isn't here!'

Mum came to look. I waved the packet of seaweed rolls at her. 'What's this?!'

'That *is* the party food, sweetiefins.'

'WHAT?!' I spluttered. 'You were supposed to buy Jiggling Jellies!'

'Well, you know that book Aunt Ditzy gave me?' Mum said. 'My inspiring thought for today was "You are what you eat".'

I stared at her in horror. 'But I don't want to be a low-fat seaweed roll!'

Mum laughed. Then she explained that it meant that if you eat healthy food you will be a healthy dolphin. I said that did **NOT** apply to parties. Mum got cross then and said that it would have to apply to this party because that was all she had bought, so I would have to like it or lump it, and blah blah blah . . . just then the phone rang. I dashed into the other room to get it.

It was Ozzie. 'Hey, guess what? Angie Angelfish gave me two Help Points yesterday for helping with her summer project!'

'That's great,' I
said.

'How's the party
planning going?'

'Great,' I said.
'Totally great. Completely
. . . grrrrrreat.'

There was a muffled **bang** and a **shriek**
from the kitchen.

'What was that noise?' said Ozzie.

'Oh, nothing, probably,' I said. There was
another bang.

'What IS going on?' asked Ozzie, alarmed.
'Do you need some help?'

'NO!' I said. 'I mean, no thank you.
Everything is under control . . .' I put the phone

down and raced into the kitchen. Mum and Myrtle were there, covered in cake.

Oh dear. The sea squirts had started exploding when they came out of the oven. Mum said they are supposed to go on *top* of the cake for decoration, not actually *in* the cake.

Not so great, then. ☹

Thought of the Day: Always follow the instructions when making cake.

SPONGEDAY

Party day! When I checked the sea-mail this
morning there was a message from the Deepsea
Divas! My heart soared – then sank like a
stonefish when I read it. They were touring
Antarctica, and wouldn't be able to come.

'Good thing you've got a Plan B,' said Dad.
He saw my face. 'No Plan B? Hmm. Well, there's
the lightshow . . .'

The phone rang. Mum answered it.

'Hello? Oh, what a shame – of course – I'll
tell her.' She put the phone down. 'That was

Gabriella from the Sparkling Sea Gooseberries. They're all in bed with tenticulitis –'

'That's it!' I wailed. 'We don't have anything for the party!'

'You've got a cake,' Dad said, encouragingly.

'A thousand bits of exploded cake!'

The phone rang again. I grabbed it – maybe the Gooseberries had miraculously recovered!

'Darcy!' It was Ozzie, and he sounded very stressed. '*Why* are there ten squillion super-sea creatures at my door at seven o'clock in the morning?!!'

Oh flippering, floundering **FISHSTICKS!** I raced to the shipwreck, to find a baying crowd of superheroes battling to get in. Myrtle and Ozzie were at the door, fending them off. I raced to help.

'What's going on?' I panted, as we managed to heave the door closed.

'The twins wrote the wrong time on the invites,' Myrtle said. 'They put 7 am instead of pm. We should have checked!'

I put my head in my fins. 'That's it!
Everything's gone wrong!'

'Why did you invite so many people?'
Ozzie asked. 'You knew I wanted a small
party!'

I flushed. 'Because ... well, I wanted to
do something big to get loads of Help Points,
and Reggie Ray said they were doing a finball

tournament, and I didn't want Reggie to win the Golden Woggle, and then I saw the poster for the jellyfish lightshow . . .'

'Jellyfish lightshow?' said Ozzie, astonished. 'We were just going to have cake and party games!'

'I know,' I said, dejectedly. 'I just got a bit . . . carried away. The lightshow isn't happening now, anyway. Or the music . . .'

'So – there's no party at all, then?' said Ozzie, slowly.

Ozzie looked horribly miserable, and then it hit me. What an idiot I'd been. It was Ozzie's birthday, and all I'd been thinking about was winning that silly Golden Woggle!

It was my fault, so I was going to have to fix things.

'Okay,' I said. 'Here's Plan B . . .'

'Happy birthday to you,

    Happy birthday to you,

    Happy birthday dear Ozzieeeeeee . . .

    Happy birthday to you!'

Ozzie, Myrtle, Diddy, Melvin Mudskipper, Ozzie's cousin Otto, the twins and I sat round Ozzie's table in the dark, as a birthday cake appeared, decorated with eight flickering plankton. It floated to the table as if by **magic!** Then Ozzie's mum appeared behind it – she'd camouflaged herself (octopuses are good at that!). Then we played Hide-n-Squeak and Pin the Tail on the Whale and ate more cake. Ozzie's mum does make ex-sea-dingly good cake! After a while I felt sick from too much cake, so I went out on the deck. A minute later, Ozzie came out too. I thought for a minute he was going to say he wasn't enjoying himself.

'Best birthday party ever,' he said. 'Thanks for helping organise it, Darcy. You're a good friend.'

A wave of happiness flooded over me.

'You know the funny thing?' I said. 'I don't care about the Golden Woggle any more. The Guppies can have it ... hang on, what's happening?!'

In the deepening blue, little pinpricks of light were appearing all over the shipwreck. At first just a few, then as we watched more and more appeared, covering the deck like a shimmering, quivering blanket! One of the lights suddenly landed on my nose.

'DOLPHIN,' it squeaked.

I stared. 'Colin?!' It was the copepod who'd caused me so much trouble when we were pet-exercising! 'How ... why ...?'

'Darcy!' Miss Batfish was swimming towards us through the twinkling lights.

'We never said thank you properly for saving Colin,' she said. 'So when we got the party invitation I thought it would be nice to do something. The lightshow was Colin's idea!'

We looked around. There must have been ten million copepods twinkling away in the darkening sea.

'You got your lightshow after all,' Ozzie said. I looked at him anxiously, thinking he'd be cross. But he grinned.

'Best lightshow ever!'

P.S. We got ten Help Points from the party guests for helping to plan the party. But we didn't win the Golden Woggle. The Guppies beat us by three points. I didn't mind. We got a special runners up prize of Jiggling Jellies, which I think made Reggie wish they'd been runners up. And more importantly, Ozzie loved his party and said I was the **best friend ever!**

Thought of the Day: Friends are better than Golden Woggles!